Margaret Deland

The Old Garden and Other Verses by Margaret Deland

Margaret Deland

The Old Garden and Other Verses by Margaret Deland

ISBN/EAN: 9783337068158

Printed in Europe, USA, Canada, Australia, Japan

Cover: Foto ©Andreas Hilbeck / pixelio.de

More available books at **www.hansebooks.com**

The Old Garden
and other verses by
Margaret Deland:
Decorated by
Walter Crane

Boston and New York
Houghton Mifflin & Co:
The Riverside Press
Cambridge · mdcccxciv

Put all thy faith in Time,
    Nor trust in me;
Grant Life, and Love, and Rhyme,
    Eternity!

To Lucy Derby.

Sweet, every rhyme here writ
  Is yours, not mine;
Your heart did dictate it,
  Mine wrote the line!
So, then, to you, whose wit
  Did make each song,
My heart and book, 't is fit
  Should both belong!

Boston, August, 1896.

Contents

The Old Garden

Nature

vii

Love Songs

Poems of Life

Verses for Children

The Old Garden

The Old Garden

O old gray house, whose broken
        casements stare
Like sad, dim eyes, at the retreating
        years,
Once more I see thee, but forlorn and bare,
And desolate of human hopes and fears.
Sagging on rusty hinges hang thy doors,
And in thy empty rooms no sound is heard
Save only when upon the echoing floors
Last autumn's drifted leaves are faintly stirred.
Braiding the darkness of the wide, bare hall,
The flick'ring sunshine softly comes and goes,
And 'gainst the broken plaster of the wall
Is blown the shadow of a climbing rose.
Oh, none but Silence and the Past, to greet
The weary heart that on the threshold stands,
Only the wind to answer eager feet,
And only shades to touch the outstretched
        hands!
The house is but poor Love's neglected grave,
While young and glad and bright with sum-
        mer's glow,

3

Like strange sweet spray upon Time's beating
    wave,
Against its grief the happy flowers grow.

Closed on three sides by crumbling walls of
    brick,
All spotted by slow-creeping lichen stains,
And nearly hid by ivy, matted thick,
And dim with clinging mists of years of rains,
The Garden lies.
              Peaceful as upland farm
That from all noise and tumult stands apart,
Yet round it is the street, a restless arm
That clasps the country to the city's heart ;
All day, outside the mildewed walls does beat
The roar of traffic and the factory's din,
The endless tramp of tired, busy feet,
Or roll of funeral car, or laugh of sin. —
Only the wall between this rush of life
And the deep quiet of this Garden old,
But yet as separate as peace and strife,
Or June's sweet sunshine from December's
    cold.

When all outside is vexed by summer rains,
Whose dash and rush will bend the stateliest
    rose,
And blur the street with dull and tearful
    stains,
The freshened Garden but the brighter glows ;

4

The swaying flowers lift their sweet, wet eyes,
And burst of perfume fills the shining air,
The drenched and dreary street feels vague
          surprise
At the strange fragrance overflowing there.
It is as though some wind of memory blew
Across the fields where earth was freshly
          ploughed,
Or over pastures dim with early dew,
Or down from hilltops hid in wreaths of cloud.
Again the drifting shadows wheel and pass
Across the roof of some far cottage home
Set where the waves of golden meadow-grass
Break with white ripples into daisy foam.
O long dead Past! O pang of strange regret —
O crimson roses bending in the rain —
Alas for hearts that may not e'en forget,
And yet would not go back to thee again!

Inside the walls, the tall ailanthus' shade
Is tangled in the meshes of the grass,
Or flecks the path, whose mossy flags were laid
For childish feet, long since grown old, to pass;
Between the stones, the scarlet pimpernel
Finds room to spread its thread-like roots and
          grow;
And all self-sown, the portulaca's bell
Lights up the ground with tender, rosy glow.
The walks are hedged with dusky green of box,
That once enclosed long borders, trim and neat;

5

Within them stood great clumps of snowy
    phlox,
That shone at dusk, and grew more deeply
    sweet.
But now the phlox wild morning-glories seek,
Whose silky blossoms robe the Garden through,
And press pure faces 'gainst the thistle's cheek,
Or star-like gleam amid the grass and dew —
A thousand pushing weeds the borders hold,
And standing with them, wild and rank as they,
Are tender blossoms, now grown over-bold,
And careless of the Garden's slow decay.
Oh, far away, in some serener air,
The eyes that loved them see a heavenly
    dawn:
How can they bloom without her tender care?
Why should they live, when her sweet life is
    gone?

Still from the far-off pastures comes the bee,
And swings all day inside the hollyhock,
Or steals her honey from the winged sweet-
    pea,
Or the striped glory of the four-o'clock;
The pale sweet-william, ringed with pink and
    white,
Grows yet within the damp shade of the wall;
And there the primrose stands, that as the
    night
Begins to gather, and the dews to fall,

Flings wide to circling moths her twisted buds,
That shine like yellow moons with pale, cold
    glow,
And all the air her heavy fragrance floods,
And gives largess to any winds that blow.

Here, in warm darkness of a night in June,
While rhythmic pulses of the factory's flame
Lighted with sudden flare of red the gloom,
And deepened long black shadows, children
    came
To watch the primrose blow !
                    Silent they stood,
Hand clasped in hand, in breathless hush
    around,
And saw her shyly doff her soft green hood
And blossom — with a silken burst of sound !

Once more I listen for the trembling chime
From purple-throated Canterbury bell ;
For surely, in that far-off golden time,
Strange fragrant music from it softly fell.
Beneath the lilacs, on whose heart-shaped leaves
The dust has settled and white stains of mould,
The money-vine with clinging myrtle weaves
A thick dark carpet, starred with blue and gold.
A wedge of vivid blue the larkspur shines
From out the thorny heart of the sweetbrier,
And at its side are velvet brandy-wines,
Shadowed by honeysuckles' fringe of fire.

7

On the long grass, where still the drops of dew
Are threaded like a necklace for the dawn,
The flaming poppies their soft petals strew,
Then stand and shiver, all their brav'ry gone.
Each crumpled, crêpe-like leaf is soft as silk;
Long, long ago the children saw them there,
Scarlet and rose, with fringes white as milk,
And called them "shawls for fairies' dainty
        wear!"
They were not finer, those laid safe away
In that low attic, 'neath the brown, warm eaves,
Where yellow sunshine on the rafters lay,
Or danced with shadows of the outside leaves —
The scent of cedarn chest in each soft fold,
And ling'ring sweetness of dried lavender,
Or pale pressed rose-leaves.

                        Still the grapevines hold
The leaning arbor, where the leaves scarce stir,
In cool green darkness that shuts out the sky;
For, if a sunbeam wandered there, 't was lost,
Or flitted like a golden butterfly
Across the ceiling that the fruit embossed.
'Neath it the path was worn and mossy green,
And here, on long, still, Sunday afternoons,
The Garden hidden by the leafy screen,
A child would walk, crooning to low, strange
        tunes,
Her catechism, or the evening hymn;
But ever gazing with a wistful eye,

8

From out the quiet of the arbor dim,
At the bright Garden, Sunday did deny.
The house is empty of the old, sweet life;
The outside world long since has claimed the
     child,
And gone forever from its bitter strife
The gentle face that always on her smiled.
Yet, though untended, still the Garden glows,
And 'gainst its walls the city's heart still beats,
And out from it each summer wind that blows
Carries some sweetness to the tired streets !

The Succory

H, not in ladies' gardens,
  My peasant Posy!
Smile thy dear, blue eyes,
  Nor only — nearer to the skies —
In upland pastures, dim and sweet —
But by the dusty road
Where tired feet
Toil to and fro;
Where flaunting Sin
May see thy heavenly hue,
Or weary Sorrow look from thee
Toward a tenderer blue!

" Butter and Eggs "

I N orange cap and yellow skirt
　　She stands — this arrant farmer
　　　　flirt !
　　　She knows the thoughts he dare
　　　　not utter,
The while he buys her eggs and butter.
He knows his fate !
And yet this silly lover begs,
　" Oh, will you sell
　A kiss, as well
As butter and eggs ? "

11

The Pansy

O dainty Pansy! hooded all in blue,
  With chastely folding cloak of green,
A maid whom Eros never knew,
  Nor Love has seen!
I yet must fancy, scarce dreamt by thee,
  That 'neath thy most discreetest thought
  There lurks a will which may be taught,
  By Love — and me!

12

The Myrtle

A. W. C.

Its clinging, mournful leaves, I said,
  Seem made to thatch a grave,
Around the roots of cypress-trees,
  Too deep in gloom for sun or breeze,
It lives to mourn the dead.

But when I kissed her name, I saw,
  Above the dear, dead maid,
A starry flower of tender blue,
A bit of heaven, shining through
  The leaves upon her grave!

The Morning-Glory

O maid!
I pray thee light,
Both noon and night;
The envious dawn
Thou lookest on
Is too soon gone;
Then stay
The day,
I pray!

14

The Sweet Pea

O H restlessly
    The gay Sweet-pea
        Nods on her slender stem;
For far up in the sunny skies
She sees the sailing butterflies,
    And longs to go to them.

For why should they
Be first to say,
    "We love thee, pretty maid"—
Why for their coming must she wait,
Nor speak of love till they dictate,
    Though Time her wings should fade?

She wonders why
She must not fly,
    Her warm heart's love to say—
Her pink and white and scarlet wings
Were surely made for better things
    Than thus at home to stay!

15

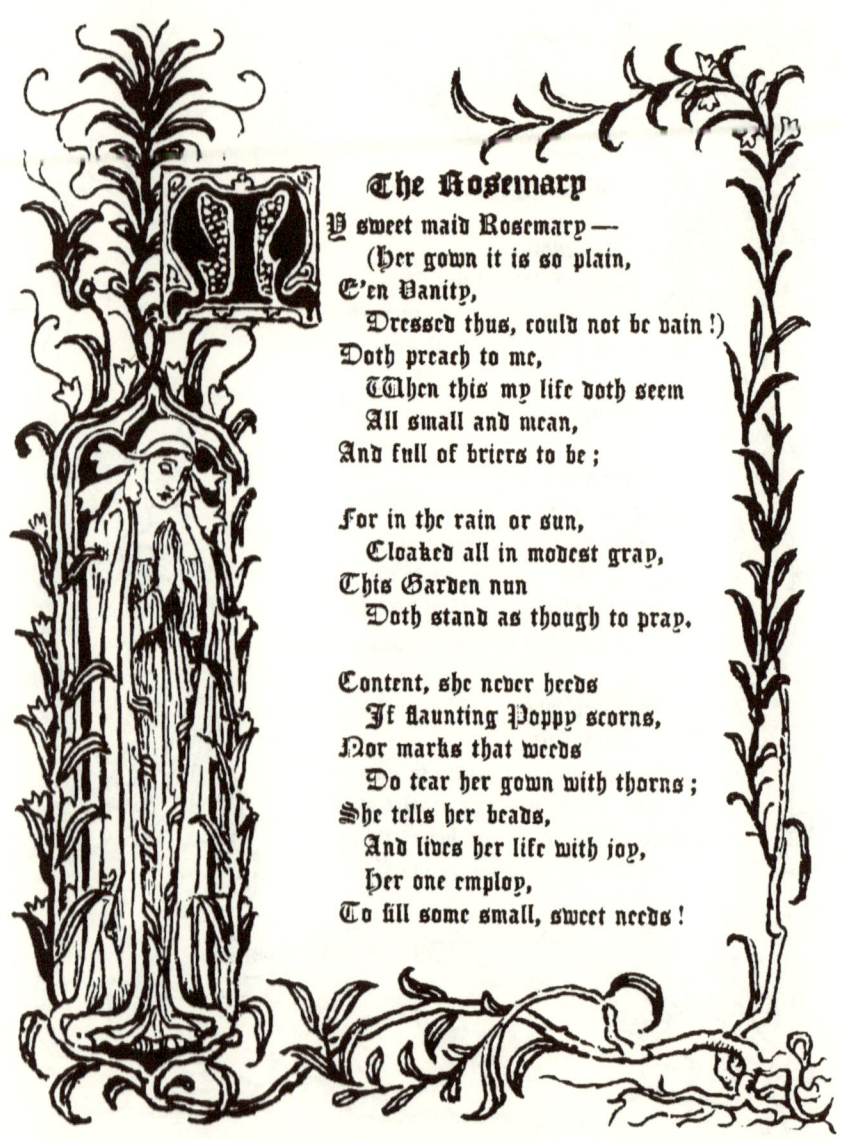

The Rosemary

MY sweet maid Rosemary —
    (Her gown it is so plain,
E'en Vanity,
    Dressed thus, could not be vain!)
Doth preach to me,
    When this my life doth seem
    All small and mean,
And full of briers to be;

For in the rain or sun,
    Cloaked all in modest gray,
This Garden nun
    Doth stand as though to pray.

Content, she never heeds
    If flaunting Poppy scorns,
Nor marks that weeds
    Do tear her gown with thorns;
She tells her beads,
    And lives her life with joy,
    Her one employ,
To fill some small, sweet needs!

The Clover

Ruddy Lover —
O brave red Clover!
Didst think to win her
Thou dost adore?
She will not love thee,
She looks above thee,
The Daisy's gold doth move her more.
If gold can win her,
Then Love's not in her;
So leave the Sinner,
And sigh no more!

17

The Yellow Daisy

What's his heart —
　　Sweetheart!
　　What's his heart?
　　Very often I 've been told
Of his yellow, shining gold;
But the gold 's the smallest part
　　Of a happy love,
　　　　Sweetheart!

Is it true,
　　My dear,
Is it true,
　　That his heart 's a rusty brown?
　　Nay, my Sweetheart! do not frown;
Better know it 's brown and sere,
Now, than when too late,
　　My dear!

18

The Bluebell

IN love she fell,
My shy Bluebell,
    With a strolling Bumble-Bee;
He whispered low,
"I love you so!
    Sweet, give your heart to me —

"I love but you,
And I'll be true,
    O give me your heart, I pray!"
She bent her head, —
"I will!" she said,
    When, lo! he flew away.

The Quaker Lady

(Houstonia Cærulea)

this quaint and quiet Quaker,
Bended head would never make her
 More discreet, or modester:
But the Gallants pass her by,
For with tender, steadfast eye,
 Straight she looks up at the sky!
Surely now, some brighter hues,
'Stead of lavenders and blues,
 Would delight some jolly fellow, —
 Russet Bee, with bands of yellow,
Or a sailing Butterfly
At her feet would love and sigh,
 Or a glow-worm trim his lamp
 When the dusk falls, cold and damp,
That its glimmering light may say,
"Dear, I love thee, Night or Day!"
 But to talk's no use, I know,
 Still in sober dress she'll go,
 And her love of heaven will show;
So, my Quaker Lady sweet,
Living in her dim retreat,
Sees no lover at her feet!

The Mignonette

A dame of high degree
        Is she,
    The gentle Mignonette —
And at her side,
    In honest pride,
Stands my sweet Bouncing Bet.

Her kerchief folded neat,
        And sweet,
Her bodice rosy-red ;
    My heart she holds
    In its soft folds,
And yet — we do not wed !

For once I raised mine eye
        Too high —
I loved fair Mignonette !
    She never knew,
    She thought me true
To humble Bouncing Bet.

Sweet hopeless Love, if wise,
        Soon dies,

And, " here 's a maid," I said ;
  " She 's lowly fair,
    And waits, — I swear," —
And yet — I do not wed !

Affaire d'Amour

For E. W. W.

One pale November day,
Flying Summer paused,
They say:
And growing bolder,
O'er rosy shoulder
Threw to her Lover such a glance,
That Autumn's heart began to dance.
(O happy Lover!)

A leafless Peach-tree bold
Thought for him she smiled,
I'm told;
And, stirred by love,
His sleeping sap did move,
Decking each naked branch with green
To show her that her look was seen!
(Alas! poor Lover!)

But Summer, laughing, fled,
Nor knew he loved her!

'Tis said
The Peach-tree sighed,
And soon he gladly died:
And Autumn, weary of the chase,
Came on at Winter's sober pace.
(O careless Lover!)

May

Like drifts of tardy snow
    On leafless branches caught,
The cherry-blossoms blow
      That May has brought.

On banks which face the sun,
    Still shy in pretty doubt,
White violets have begun
      To look about;

The fresh winds gayly bring
    The orchards' faint perfume,
And purple lilacs swing
      Their feathery bloom!

Along the meadow's edge
    New grass has just been seen,
And on the hawthorn hedge
      Rose hides the green.

Sunshine lies warm and still:
    Cloud shadows idly drift:
Light cups, for dews to fill,
      Wind-flowers lift;

Oh, sweet, fresh world, and young!
A bluebird flashes by,
And singing joy is flung
Through all the sky!

The Wild Rose

Since on my suit, alas!
  My Lady dear doth frown,
I lay where she may pass,
  A wild Rose down.

But first, lest it should grieve
  Thus to be laid so low,
Into its heart I breathe
  All my heart's woe:

" Her nature is so sweet,
  (Save only unto me!)
Even her little feet
  Will not wound thee;

" Where thine own color glows,
  Warm on her dainty cheek,
She 'll lift thee, happy Rose!
  Then, dear Rose, Speak!

" My intercessor be,
  And in her tiny ear
Whisper — ' he loveth thee,
  Who sent me, dear ! ' "

June

Upon the breast of smiling June
   Roses and lilies lie,
And round her yet is faint perfume
   Of violets, just gone by;

Green is her gown, with 'broidery
   Of blossoming meadow grass,
That ripples like a flowing sea
   When winds and shadows pass.

Her breast is belted by the blue
   Of succory, like the sky,
And purple heart's-ease clasp her too,
   And larkspur growing high;

Laced is her bodice green with vines,
   And dew the sun has kissed,
Jewels her scarf that faintly shines,
   In folds of morning mist!

The buttercups are fringes fair
   Around her small white feet,
And on the radiance of her hair
   Fall cherry-blossoms sweet;

30

The dark laburnum's chains of gold
  She twists about her throat:
Perched on her shoulder, blithe and bold,
  The brown thrush sounds his note!

And blue of the far dappled sky
  That shows at warm, still noon,
Shines in her softly smiling eye —
  Oh! who's so sweet as June?

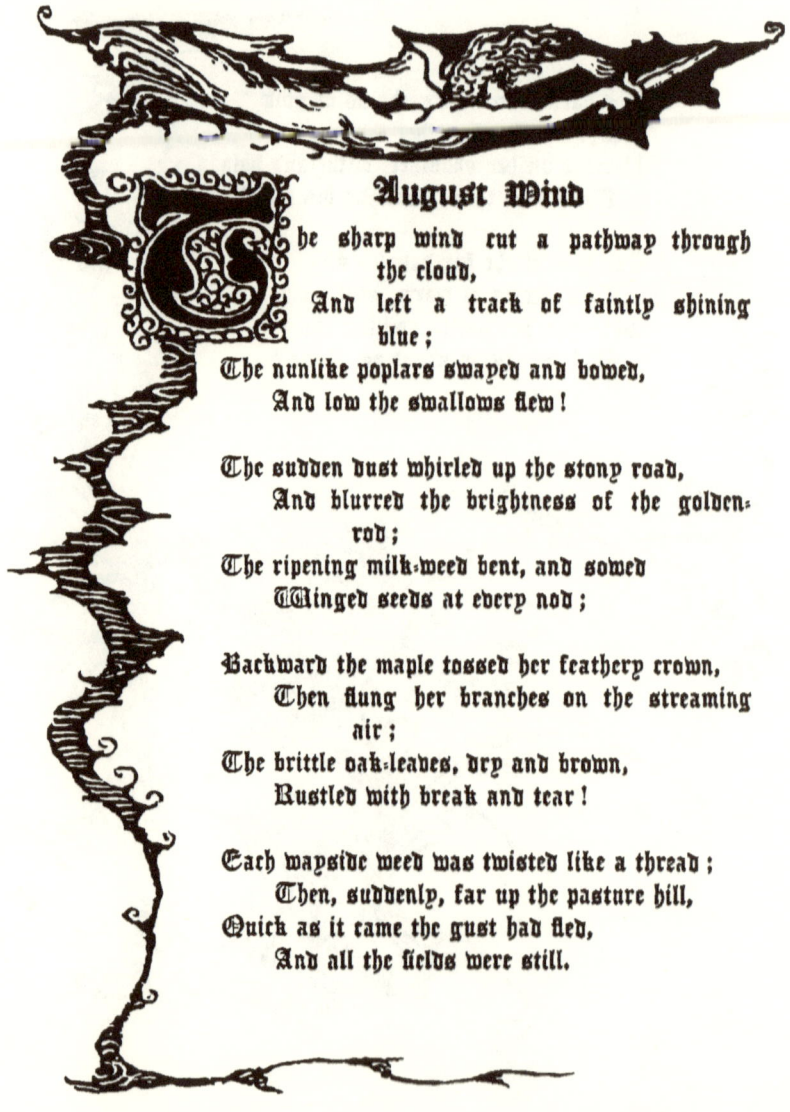

August Wind

The sharp wind cut a pathway through
the cloud,
And left a track of faintly shining
blue;
The nunlike poplars swayed and bowed,
And low the swallows flew!

The sudden dust whirled up the stony road,
And blurred the brightness of the golden-
rod;
The ripening milk-weed bent, and sowed
Winged seeds at every nod;

Backward the maple tossed her feathery crown,
Then flung her branches on the streaming
air;
The brittle oak-leaves, dry and brown,
Rustled with break and tear!

Each wayside weed was twisted like a thread;
Then, suddenly, far up the pasture hill,
Quick as it came the gust had fled,
And all the fields were still.

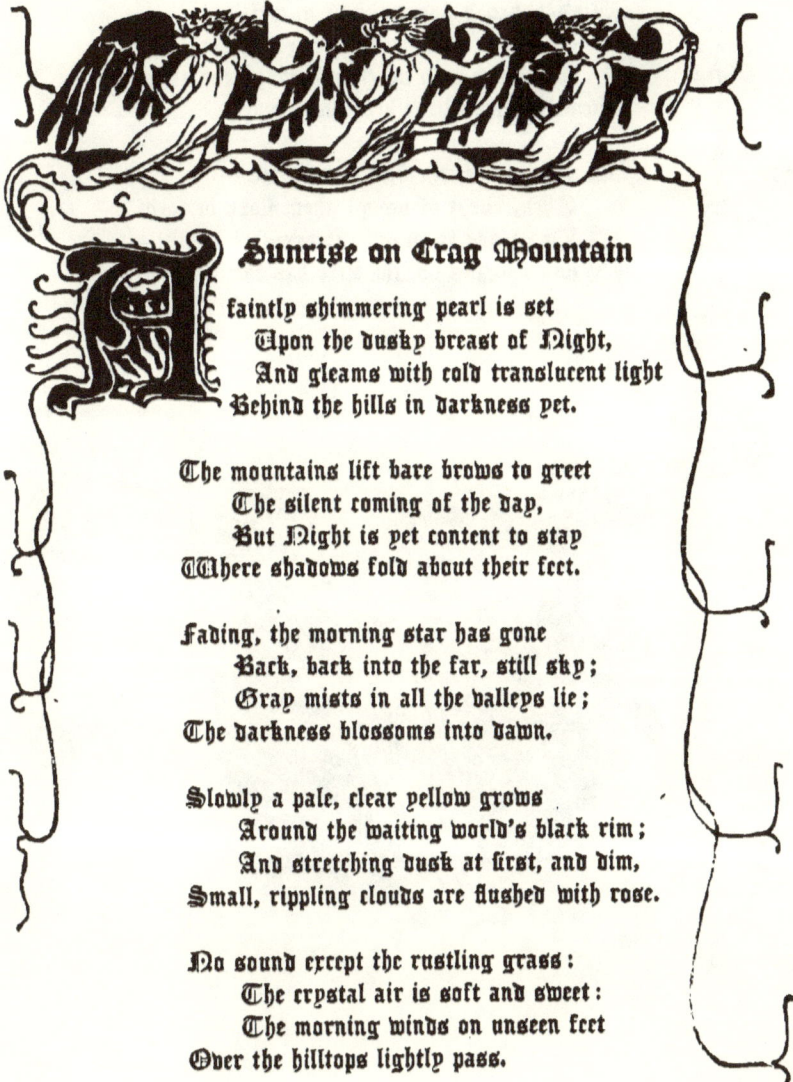

Sunrise on Crag Mountain

A faintly shimmering pearl is set
    Upon the dusky breast of Night,
    And gleams with cold translucent light
Behind the hills in darkness yet.

The mountains lift bare brows to greet
    The silent coming of the day,
    But Night is yet content to stay
Where shadows fold about their feet.

Fading, the morning star has gone
    Back, back into the far, still sky;
    Gray mists in all the valleys lie;
The darkness blossoms into dawn.

Slowly a pale, clear yellow grows
    Around the waiting world's black rim;
    And stretching dusk at first, and dim,
Small, rippling clouds are flushed with rose.

No sound except the rustling grass:
    The crystal air is soft and sweet:
    The morning winds on unseen feet
Over the hilltops lightly pass.

Wind-wakened flowers, half uncurled,
   Turn to the East their eager eyes;
   A pulsing gold spreads through the skies —
Silence wraps all the breathless world.

One moment yet the birds are dumb —
   Then, burst of song! then, flood of light!
   Day leaps from out the arms of Night —
The sun springs up, the Life has come!

34

Hepatica

A pretty, modest maid
Who still is half afraid
   Of chilly winter weather,
But yet is all too shy
To boldly search the sky,
   To see if storm-clouds gather.

So, in some dim, still place,
Has hid her small, sweet face,
   And let dead leaves drift round her;
And bent her head so low,
Not softest winds that blow,
   Nor sunshine, scarce have found
      her;

She wears a hood of green,
(So fears she to be seen,)
   And folds about her neatly,
A simple russet gown
Of furry leaves and brown,
   That hides her form completely;

Will she thus live and fade,
Poor, pretty, modest maid!
   If she her beauty covers?´

35

Nay, for though other eyes
Note not where low she lies,
    She can't escape her Lover's!

He 'll search the damp woods through
To find the tender blue
    Of her eyes, shyly smiling,
Nor heed the wet and cold,
Where dead leaves drift and fold,
    Her look is so beguiling!

The Golden-Rod

O rod of gold!
O swaying sceptre of the year —
Now frost and cold
Show Winter near,
And shivering leaves grow brown and sere.
The bleak hillside,
And marshy waste of yellow reeds,
And meadows wide
Where frosted weeds
Shake on the damp wind light-winged seeds,
Are decked with thee, —
The lingering Summer's latest grace,
And sovereignty.
Each wind-swept space
Waves thy red gold in Winter's face —
He strives each star,
In stormy pride to lay full low;
But when thy bar
Resists his blow,
Will crown thee with a puff of snow!

37

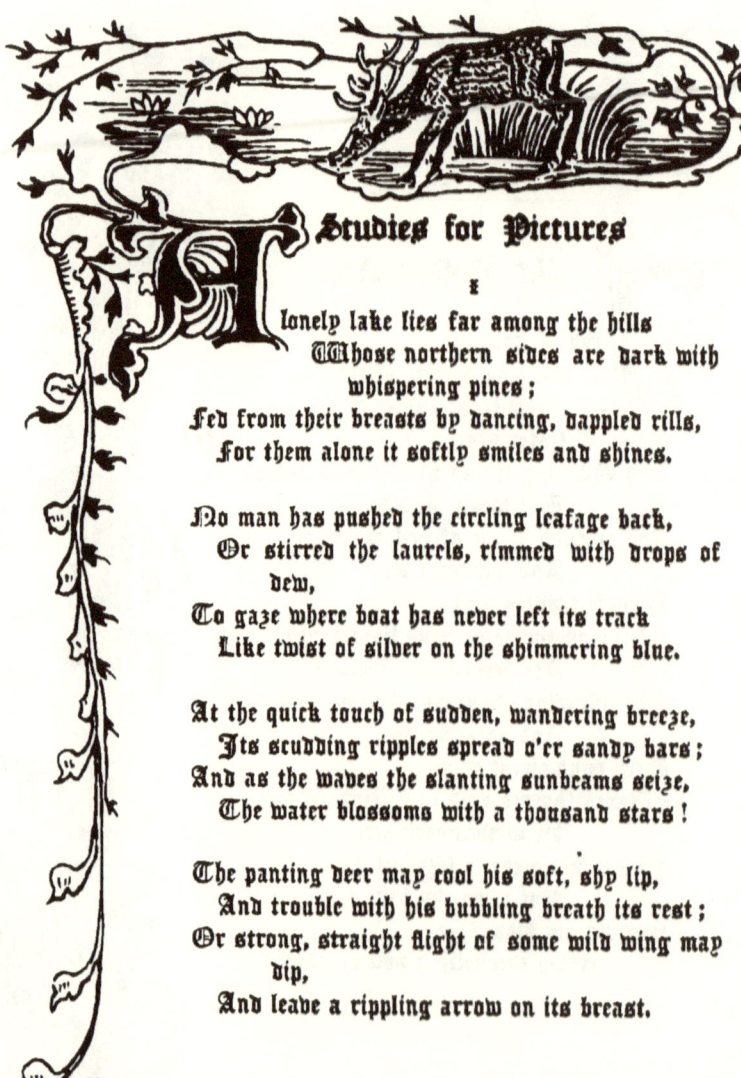

Studies for Pictures

I

A lonely lake lies far among the hills
  Whose northern sides are dark with
    whispering pines;
Fed from their breasts by dancing, dappled rills,
  For them alone it softly smiles and shines.

No man has pushed the circling leafage back,
  Or stirred the laurels, rimmed with drops of
    dew,
To gaze where boat has never left its track
  Like twist of silver on the shimmering blue.

At the quick touch of sudden, wandering breeze,
  Its scudding ripples spread o'er sandy bars;
And as the waves the slanting sunbeams seize,
  The water blossoms with a thousand stars!

The panting deer may cool his soft, shy lip,
  And trouble with his bubbling breath its rest;
Or strong, straight flight of some wild wing may
    dip,
  And leave a rippling arrow on its breast.

With sharp, green spears, the reeds and grasses
    pierce
The still dark water 'neath o'erhanging trees,
As though some Pharaoh's army, wild and
    fierce,
    Were buried, marching, as in Egypt's seas!

Over its heart it folds a scarf of lace, —
    Faint-imaged clouds that stretch across the
    sky, —
And, like white jewels fastening it in place,
    The trembling-hearted water-lilies lie.

It braids the moonbeams on a summer night,
    Or, while low laughter all its bosom fills,
Its ripples chase the west wind's sunny flight,
    And kiss the feet of its grave, guarding hills!

II

Like heavy stream of slow, scarce-moving oil,
    On open flats the dim, still river lies;
No skimming ripple, and no whirling coil
    Of dimpling eddy, stirs its mirrored skies;

No bending grasses on the sandy shore
    Reach their long fingers down to dip and
    lave;
And all unmarked the river's even floor
    By hidden pebbles' softly slipping wave.

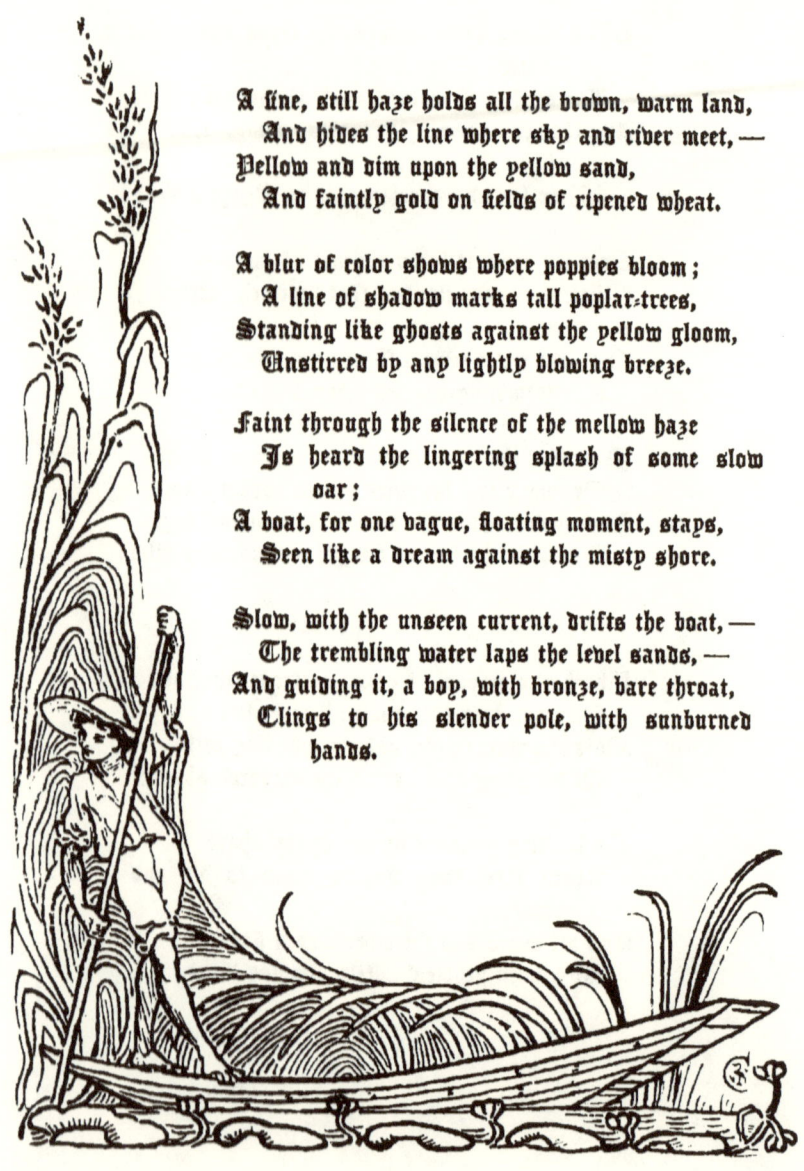

A fine, still haze holds all the brown, warm land,
   And hides the line where sky and river meet, —
Yellow and dim upon the yellow sand,
   And faintly gold on fields of ripened wheat.

A blur of color shows where poppies bloom;
   A line of shadow marks tall poplar-trees,
Standing like ghosts against the yellow gloom,
   Unstirred by any lightly blowing breeze.

Faint through the silence of the mellow haze
   Is heard the lingering splash of some slow
      oar;
A boat, for one vague, floating moment, stays,
   Seen like a dream against the misty shore.

Slow, with the unseen current, drifts the boat, —
   The trembling water laps the level sands, —
And guiding it, a boy, with bronze, bare throat,
   Clings to his slender pole, with sunburned
      hands.

The Night Mist

ALL the night long, the gray embracing mist
  Has held in tender arms the tired
    world;
The sleepy river its soft lips have kissed,
  And over hills and meadows it has curled.

Its white cool finger it has gently placed
  On weary stretches of the desert sand;
The noisy city, and the far-off waste,
  Have felt the benediction of its hand.

The drowsy world rolls slowly toward the day:
  The fresh sweet wind of morning softly blows:
The willing mist no longer now may stay;
  With first expectancy of dawn, it goes!

41

Bloodroot Blossoms

When shiv'ring through the skies,
 Spring sought the wintry earth,
She saw with longing eyes
The gleaming stars arise
 To light her chilly path!

She might not wait or stay,
 To pluck them for a crown,
For dim and far away
The world expectant lay,
 And she must hasten down;

But there, for necklace bright
 With soft cold hands she made
Some stars, all snowy white,
Gleaming like those of night,
 And on her young breast laid.

So, on Spring's bosom cold,
 These starry blossoms glow,
Half hid by many a fold
Of brown leaves, sere and old,
 And sodden by past snow!

42

Spring's Beacon

Through the misty woodlands bare,
　By the meadows brown and dead,
　　In the damp and chilly air,
　　Stand the maples tipped with red;

They are flaring signals bright,
　Wav'ring 'gainst the dull, cold sky,
Heralding with ruddy light,
　That the cheerful Spring is nigh.

In their kindling, flaming boughs,
　Wooing Robins love and sing,
Swearing all their pretty vows,
　"By the Beacon of the Spring!"

Crimson on the Robin's breast,
　Crimson on the growing tree —
Life and Love alike are drest,
　Love and Life have come to me!

Crimson on my Love's soft cheeks
　Does her sweet, shy thought confess,
When from out her heart she speaks,
　To my heart the longed-for — "Yes!"

Summer

A Fragment

High on the crest of the blossoming
grasses,
Bending and swaying with face toward
the sky,
Stirred by the lightest west wind as it passes,
Hosts of the silver-white daisy-stars lie!

I, looking up through the mists of the flowers,
I, lying low on the earth thrilled with June,
Give not a thought to the vanishing hours,
Save that they melt into twilight too soon!

Blossoms of peaches float down for my cover, —
Snow-flakes that blushed to be kissed by the
sun, —
Blossoms of apples drift over and over, —
White they with grief that their short day is
done!

Buttercup's lanterns are lighted about me,
Burly red clover's warm cheek presses mine;
Powdery Bee never once seems to doubt me,
Tipping each chalice for Summer's new wine!

Tiny white butterflies ("Brides" children name
  them)
Flicker and glimmer, and turn in their flight;
Surely the sunshine suffices to tame them,
  Close to my hand they will swing and alight!

Small timid breezes, than butterflies shyer,
  Just for a moment soft buffet my face,
Then fly away to the tree-tops and higher,
  Shaking down shadows o'er every bright space.

Love Songs

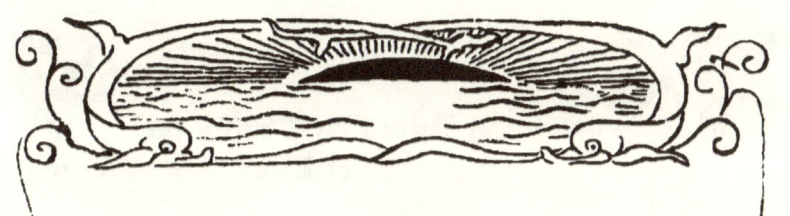

To Thee

L. F. D.

O thou Beloved! in whose eyes I read
A ready strength to meet my utmost
    need,
I ponder, sometimes (noting thy content
With this small life of mine, which thou hast
    bent
To all of lofty purpose it can claim
By thine uplifting praise, or tender blame),
I wonder, sometimes, hast thou ever thought
How with thyself my conscious life is wrought?
That thou the centre art, the clasp and stay
Of Past, and Future, and the glad To-day!
As dim horizon binds a shoreless sea,
My widening life is bound and arched by thee;
And, lighting all this heaven that holds my heart,
Gladness, and joy, and warmth, and sun, thou
    art!

On being Asked by Phyllis for a Picture of Love

Gray are Love's gentle eyes,
    And in them stay
Sweet thoughts, and wise:
This sure no one denies,
    For Phyllis' eyes are gray.

Red is Love's mouth, as though
    On roses fed:
This do I know,
Since Phyllis' lips do show
    A like sweet damask=red.

Brown is Love's hair, and bright,
    And soft as down,
And curling light
Around a forehead white,
    And Phyllis' hair is brown.

Sweet is true Love, but shy
    As a young dove
Just taught to fly —
All this right well know I,
    For Phyllis is my Love!

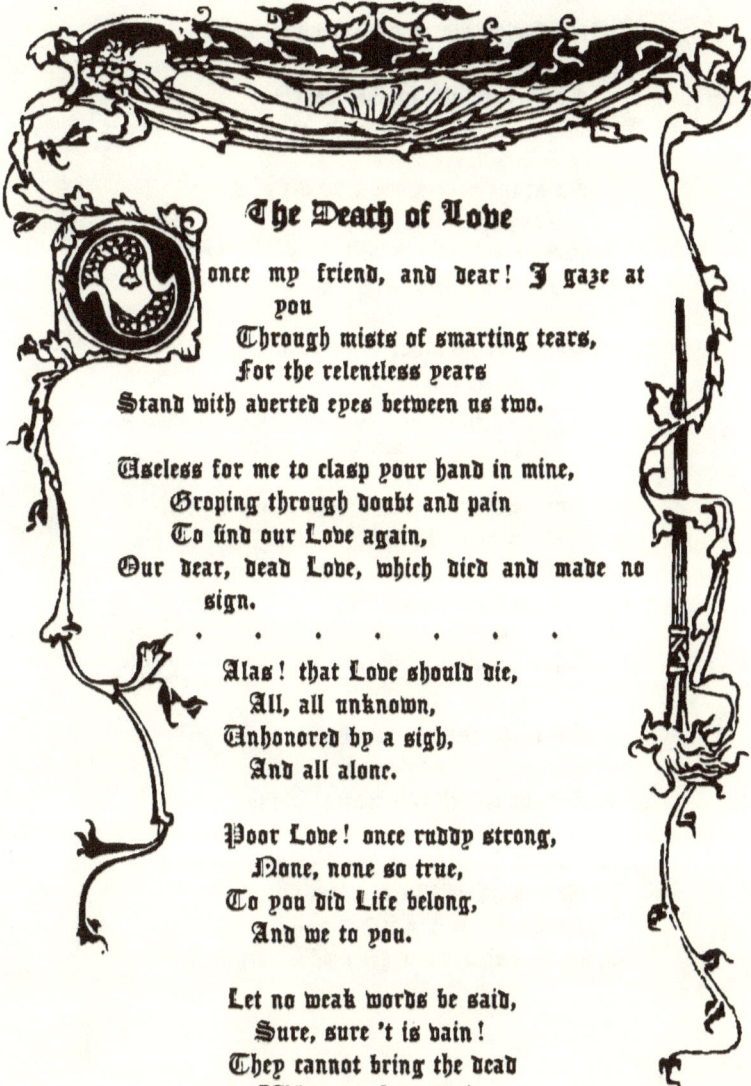

The Death of Love

Once my friend, and dear! I gaze at you
　　　you
　　Through mists of smarting tears,
　　For the relentless years
Stand with averted eyes between us two.

Useless for me to clasp your hand in mine,
　　Groping through doubt and pain
　　To find our Love again,
Our dear, dead Love, which died and made no
　　sign.

　　　•　•　•　•　•　•　•

　　Alas! that Love should die,
　　　All, all unknown,
　　Unhonored by a sigh,
　　　And all alone.

　　Poor Love! once ruddy strong,
　　　None, none so true,
　　To you did Life belong,
　　　And we to you.

　　Let no weak words be said,
　　　Sure, sure 't is vain!
　　They cannot bring the dead
　　　Whom we have slain.

51

Useless for us old tender words to speak;
    As well to try to bring
    The breath of vanished Spring,
Or glory of a rose, long dead, to seek.

    So grant poor Love a decent grave
      And cereclothes, too,
    And deck his head with blossoms brave,
      Dark pansies, mixed with rue!

    But carve no stone to mark his bed,
      Or show his name;
    Enough for us our Love is dead,
      Why tell the world our shame?

    Poor murdered Love! this sharp regret,
      This grief, is well.
    But shall Grief live, or we forget?
      Alas! we cannot tell.

Yes, even this our Grief, which takes Love's
      throne,
    On some unconscious day
    Unseen may slip away,
And Self be left in full content alone.

Poor human hearts, not great enough to wear
    Remembrance like a crown:
    Glad soon to lay it down —
Oh, sharper this, than grief of Death to bear!

To Jealousie

Jealousie!
    I welcome thee
    To stab my patient breast,
    For such a guest
Is sure some day to prove
To her my gentle love, —
How great my love must be
To harbor thee!

But that my pain
Be not endured in vain,
    I must with nicest art
    Disclose thy dart,
So that her eye may see
My misery,
    And her most tender heart
    Be moved to heal thy smart.

For this, I suffer thee,
O Jealousie!

53

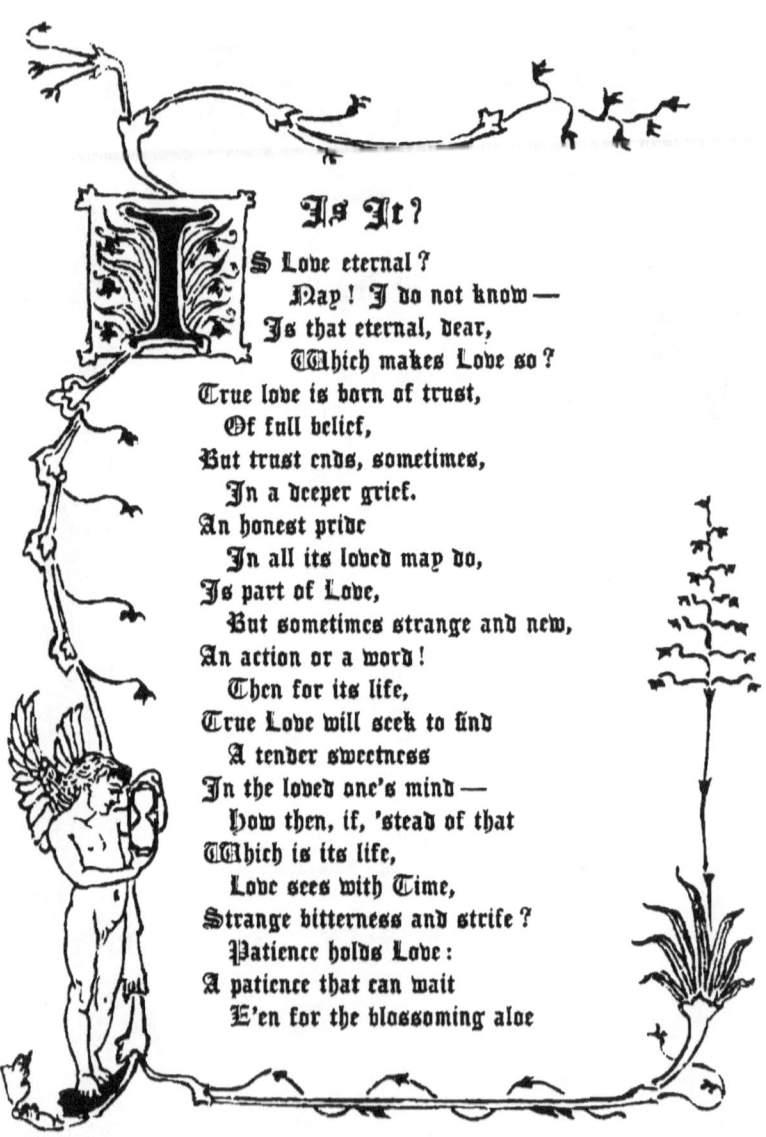

Is It?

IS Love eternal?
　　Nay! I do not know—
　Is that eternal, dear,
　　Which makes Love so?
True love is born of trust,
　Of full belief,
But trust ends, sometimes,
　In a deeper grief.
An honest pride
　In all its loved may do,
Is part of Love,
　But sometimes strange and new,
An action or a word!
　Then for its life,
True Love will seek to find
　A tender sweetness
In the loved one's mind—
　How then, if, 'stead of that
Which is its life,
　Love sees with Time,
Strange bitterness and strife?
　Patience holds Love:
A patience that can wait
　E'en for the blossoming aloe

Of its fate —
   Which bears a passing shadow
In Love's eyes,
   Nay, if they turn from it,
Knows no surprise,
   Owning its own unworth!
Then, if Love's heart
   Beats only while it trusts,
And finds it part
   In tenderness,
And glows with pride,
   And sees sweet patience
Ever at its side —
   Then Love will only last
As long as they —
   " Is love eternal ? "
That 's for you to say!

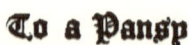

To a Pansy

N such modest wise she stands,
　My sweet purple Pansy flower!
That she all my heart commands —
　Prithee, does she know her power?

Tell me, does she look so shy,
　Just to make me love her so?
If she does, I swear that I
　Half her charm did never know!

For such strategies avow
　That within her heart Love stirs,
And perhaps she'll welcome now
　What, unknown to her, is hers!

56

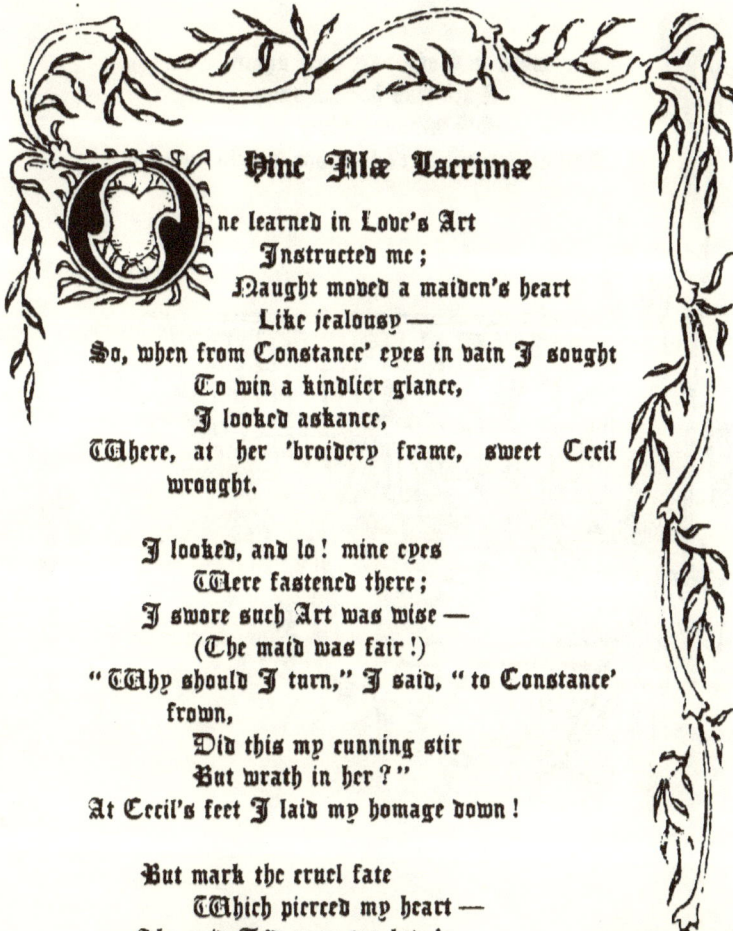

Hinc Illæ Lacrimæ

One learned in Love's Art
    Instructed me;
  Naught moved a maiden's heart
    Like jealousy —
So, when from Constance' eyes in vain I sought
  To win a kindlier glance,
    I looked askance,
Where, at her 'broidery frame, sweet Cecil
  wrought.

  I looked, and lo! mine eyes
    Were fastened there;
  I swore such Art was wise —
    (The maid was fair!)
"Why should I turn," I said, "to Constance'
  frown,
    Did this my cunning stir
    But wrath in her?"
At Cecil's feet I laid my homage down!

  But mark the cruel fate
    Which pierced my heart —
  She said I'd come too late!
    I cursed the Art —

For, when to Constance once again I turned,
　　Such was her jealousy
　　She 'd none of me,
And all my proffered love she lightly spurned!

58

A Lover to His Mistress

Surely, dear, the wild brown Bee,
  When he sees your ruddy lip,
Flutters near that he may see
  If it blooms for him to sip!

Sunbeams of the dawning day
  Note your curls' soft golden gleam
And are tangled there, and stay,
  For they sister sunbeams seem;

And I know the butterflies,
  Sailing through the fragrant air,
Mark the heaven of your eyes,
  And must long to enter there!

And the wanton wind which blows
  Soft from out the yellow west,
Stays a moment to repose
  On the whiteness of your breast; —

But such longing fills my soul,
  When mine eyes such beauties see,
I would fain possess the whole,
  Nor would share with Wind or Bee!

Arrière Pensée

IT was not Love, you know,
 That dream of ours :
No doubt we thought it so,
Catching the shine and glow
 From sun and sky and flowers !

"I called it Love!" you say ?
 What if I did ?
The words but matched the day,
It died, and so should they,
 None surely could forbid ;

"Love never dies," you swear ?
 "Love such as yours ; "
Well, that must be your care,
To blame me is not fair,
 Because your pain endures ;

I'm really sorry I
 Should seem unkind !
But you cannot deny
The Summer's long gone by ;
 'T was time to change my mind ;

60

Indeed, it's wiser, far,
    To take my view:
Love always leaves a scar,
We're better as we are,
    And friendship will be new!

Uncertainty

The distant ships at anchor lie
    Far on the hazy sea;
        Upon the helm we see no hand,
        Nor hear a whisper of command;
    Our own they seem to be.

    Under a tender sky they rest,
        With snowy sails all furled;
        But the mist may lift,
        And the wind may shift,
    And the ships sail down the world!

    Oh, the sweet souls I truly love
        Shall I ever truly know?
        In their mists of thought,
        I am all untaught,
    Nor know I what winds may blow!

"Many Waters cannot Quench Love"

Shall earthly Love, which so to heaven belongs
    That she may lay her hand upon God's throne,
Or join the morning stars' immortal songs,
    Know all serenest heights, but heights alone?

Shall hers be knowledge of supremest joy,
    Fullness of fame and honor all be hers —
Perfected sweetness, which may never cloy,
    A rose unruffled, though the west wind stirs!

Shall she know only calm, with high content
    To live each day in blaze of searching light —
Is this alone for Love? If heaven be rent
    And drown her dazzled eyes in outer night:

If honor die; if she is stripped of Fame;
    If that fair rose is scattered by the rain,
Broken, and stained, its beauty turned to shame —
    Shall this be hid from Love? Then Life were vain!

Not only heights and sweetness Love must
        know,
    Nor only lean upon the throne of God:
Depths too are hers, and sometimes, bending
        low,
    She kisses feet that deeps of sin have trod;

Against the dust she lays her stately head,
    Or bares her heart to blasting storms and
        rain;
Patient she follows wheresoever led,
    Nor recks of darkness, weariness, and pain!

She may not even raise her eyes for tears,
    And sighs instead of songs chain every breath;
For lo! a crown of lead and gold she wears,
    Life's circle, clasping the black pearl of Death!

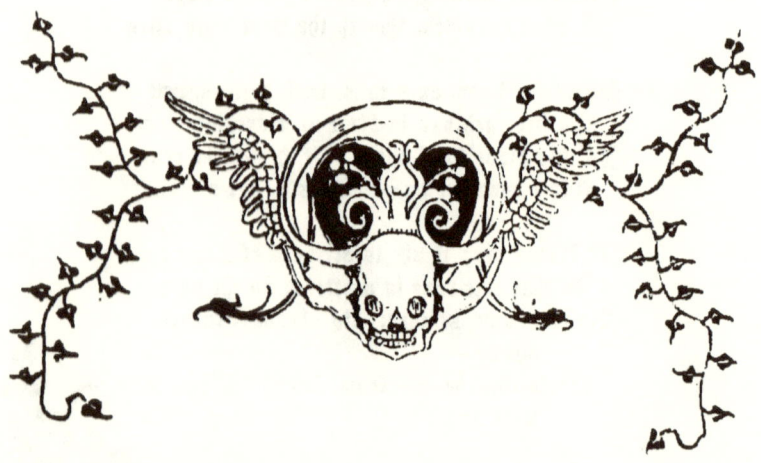

On Presenting a Scentless Rose to a Young Gentlewoman

ALL thy soft leaves, fair Rose! are silky
      fine,
      And cool —
      But I — poor fool!
Looked for hot passion in this heart of thine,
      So deeply red;
      Instead
I did but find
      It set about with thorn,
      And scentless quite!
The which when I my tired head would bind
      With its delight,
      Left me but more forlorn!
Better, dear hypocrite,
      Thou shouldst e'en thy fair looks deny
      To such as I,
Since the sweet meaning in them writ
      Is but a lie!

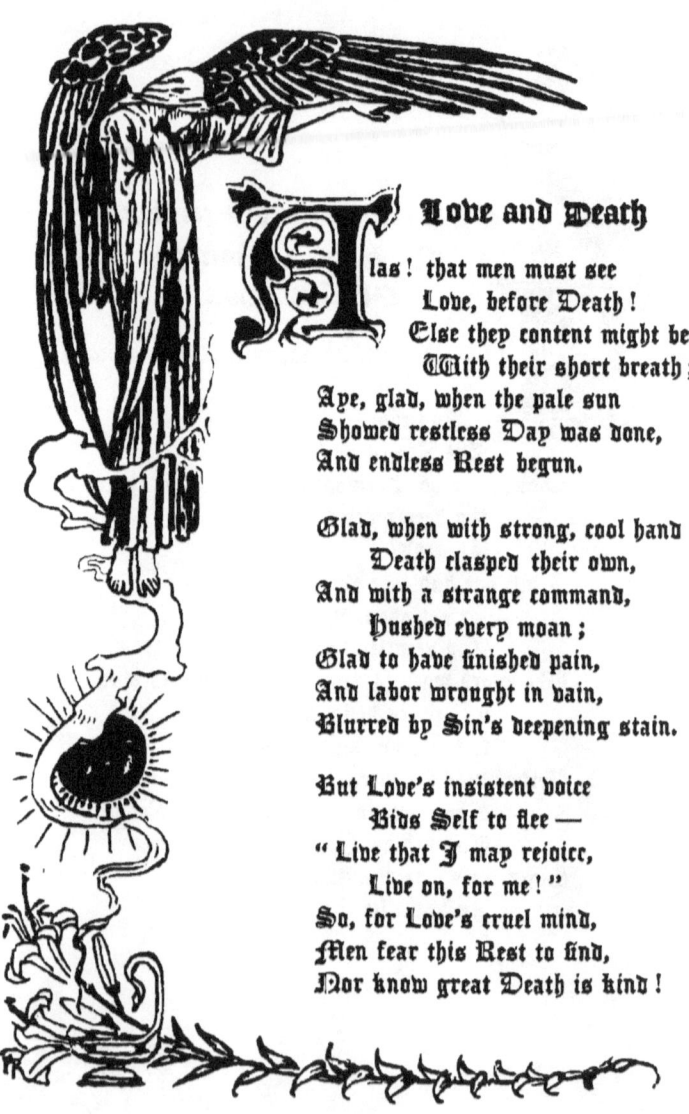

Love and Death

Alas! that men must see
　　Love, before Death!
　　Else they content might be
　　With their short breath;
Aye, glad, when the pale sun
Showed restless Day was done,
And endless Rest begun.

Glad, when with strong, cool hand
　　Death clasped their own,
And with a strange command,
　　Hushed every moan;
Glad to have finished pain,
And labor wrought in vain,
Blurred by Sin's deepening stain.

But Love's insistent voice
　　Bids Self to flee —
"Live that I may rejoice,
　　Live on, for me!"
So, for Love's cruel mind,
Men fear this Rest to find,
Nor know great Death is kind!

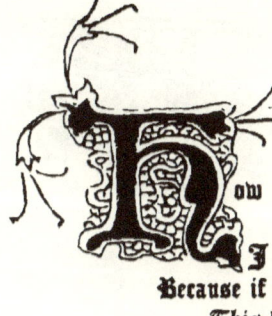

Love's Wisdom

How long I've loved thee, and how
    well —
        I dare not tell!
Because if thou shouldst once divine
    This love of mine,
Or did but once my tongue confess
    My heart's distress,
Far, far too plainly thou wouldst see
    My slavery,
And, guessing what Love's wit should hide,
    Rest satisfied!

So, though I worship at thy feet,
    I'll be discreet —
And all my love shall not be told,
    Lest thou be cold,
And, knowing I was always thine,
    Scorn to be mine.
So am I dumb, to rescue thee
    From tyranny —
And, by my silence, I do prove
    Wisdom and Love!

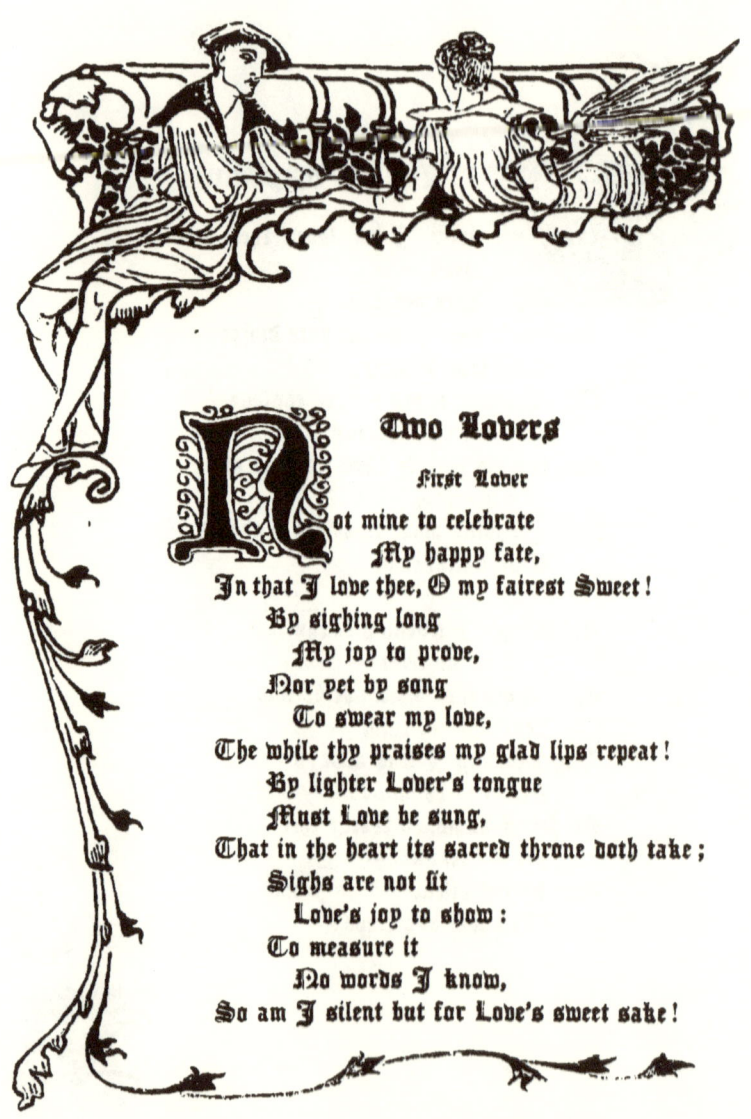

Two Lovers

First Lover

Not mine to celebrate
My happy fate,
In that I love thee, O my fairest Sweet!
By sighing long
My joy to prove,
Nor yet by song
To swear my love,
The while thy praises my glad lips repeat!
By lighter Lover's tongue
Must Love be sung,
That in the heart its sacred throne doth take;
Sighs are not fit
Love's joy to show:
To measure it
No words I know,
So am I silent but for Love's sweet sake!

Second Lover

That I have words wherewith to speak
    my love,
    Doth never argue that my love is
    weak,
   But rather prove
  That I do gain a grace
  From her fair face,
Which, nurturing gracious words, bids me to
    speak:
The endless music that her living makes
  Through weary days, and every day, to me,
    My song awakes;
   But it doth start my sighs
   That her sweet eyes
The often baseness of my life must see!

Inconstancy

You ask me does Love's flame
  Burn still the same,
    And if unchanged quite,
  It cheers
    The lengthening years
  With soft and tender light;
If it yet shows the old, warm, ruddy glow?
And I must answer — "No!"

It is not still the same,
Yet spare me blame!
  For, though to change be wrong,
    It will
    Be changing still,
  To grow each day more strong!
Can you such sweet, inconstant Love confess?
I pray you answer — "Yes!"

70

Lines to a Very Shy Young Woman

False Violet, I sought for thee,
  That I might know,
    If thou didst bend so low,
Prompted by tender modesty,
    Or show!

I will disclose thy subtlety : —
  Looks that are shy,
    Thou know'st do win mine eye —
(This truth, fair maid, I challenge thee,
    Deny!)

And so, since it becometh thee,
  And charms my heart —
    Thou dost affect this part,
Thus, all thy sweet simplicity
    Is Art!

Love's Coup D'Etat

No longer at thy feet,
　My only Dear,
　　With honied words I'll woo thee!
Nor ever fear
That with thy praises sweet,
　I will again pursue thee.

"Soft stars of night," thine eyes
　Did folly call,
　　To make thee smile upon me.
Love's favor small!
Instead, thou didst chastise
　With frowns, and yet more shun me.

So, now 'tis time to try,
　Truth to thy mind:
　　Thou seest not that I love thee?
Then art thou blind!
'Tis sin to say thine eye
　Is like a star above thee.

"Thy lips were made to kiss,"
　Long time I said,

Though thou'st with scorn denied me
To taste their red —
Know that they speak amiss
    When they do thus deride me.

"The dimple in thy chin
  For Love was made?"
      Alas, I did not know thee.
    That trap was laid
  To catch my heart within,
    As I — a fool — did show thee.

"Thine heart was sweet and true,"
  Once wert thou told.
      Now, Lady, prithee hear me:
    Thine heart is cold!
(Such words are surely new,
    Truth, haply, may endear me.)

One thing I cannot say, —
  Loving sweet Truth, —
      Though fain I would abuse thee
    With words of ruth —
That there can dawn a day
    My heart will cease to choose thee!

Sent with a Rose, to a Young Lady

Deep in a Rose's glowing heart
    I dropped a single kiss,
And then I bade it quick depart,
    And tell my Lady this:

"The love thy Lover tried to send
    O'erflows my fragrant bowl,
But my soft leaves would break and bend,
    Should he send half the whole!"

On being Reproached by my Love for Coldness

Dearest, I cannot say "I love but thee,"
    Nor yet deny
    My roving eye
Does other beauty see!

But from one cause do these shortcomings
    spring:
    So fair thou art
    My captive heart
Sees thee in everything:

So, why I do not love but thee is plain,
    The whole world's dear
    While thou art here,—
While thee it does contain!

And why to beauty I'm not blind is clear:
    On every face
    Some of thy grace
To my eye doth appear.

But though sweet nothings, true, J cannot say,
Yet thee J love
My life above,
So love me, dear, J pray!

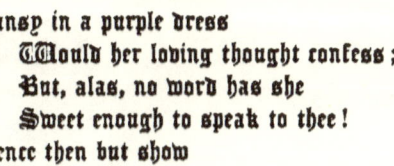

Verses

Pansy in a purple dress
Would her loving thought confess;
But, alas, no word has she
Sweet enough to speak to thee!
Let her silence then but show
Depth of love you do not know.

The Love that hides, too modest far to speak —
Is sometimes twice as strong, for seeming
weak:
Hear then, what these my pansies say to you —
"Your Lover, dear, is shy, but always true!"

77

Life

By one great Heart the Universe is
    stirred :
    By Its strong pulse, stars climb the
      darkening blue ;
It throbs in each fresh sunset's changing
    hue,
And thrills through low sweet song of every
    bird :

By It, the plunging blood reds all men's veins ;
    Joy feels that heart against his rapturous
      own,
    And on It, Sorrow breathes her sharpest
      groan ;
It bounds through gladnesses and deepest
    pains.

Passionless beating through all Time and Space,
    Relentless, calm, majestic in Its march,
    Alike, though Nature shake heaven's endless
      arch,
Or man's heart break, because of some dead
    face !

'T is felt in sunshine greening the soft sod,
   In children's smiling, as in mother's tears;
   And, for strange comfort, through the aching
      years,
Men's hungry souls have named that great Heart,
      God!

Death

Into the land that no man knows,
    Into the darkness that may mean
        light,
        Shaken with doubt the poor Soul goes,
    Hoping the blindness of Death brings sight;

Out of a mystery it grew,
    And life was a riddle hard to read;
Can Death show joy it never knew,
    Or to full knowledge gently lead?

That awful Face may turn and smile,
    When on Its lips our own we lay—
Saying, "Trust me a little while,
    Fear not the Night that brings the Day!"

Doubt

O distant Christ, the crowded, darkening
    years
    Drift slow between thy gracious face
    and me:
My hungry heart leans back to look for thee,
But finds the way set thick with doubts and
    fears.

My groping hands would touch thy garment's
    hem,
    Would find some token thou art walking near;
    Instead, they clasp but empty darkness drear,
And no diviner hands reach out to them.

Sometimes my listening soul, with bated breath,
    Stands still to catch a footfall by my side,
    Lest, haply, my earth-blinded eyes but hide
Thy stately figure, leading Life and Death;

My straining eyes, O Christ, but long to mark
    A shadow of thy presence, dim and sweet,

Or far-off light to guide my wandering feet,
Or hope for hands prayer-beating 'gainst the
    dark.

O Thou! unseen by me, that like a child
    Tries in the night to find its mother's heart,
    And weeping wanders only more apart,
Not knowing in the darkness that she smiled—

Thou, all unseen, dost hear my tired cry,
    As I, in darkness of a half belief,
    Grope for thy heart, in love and doubt and
        grief:
O Lord! speak soon to me—"Lo, here am I!"

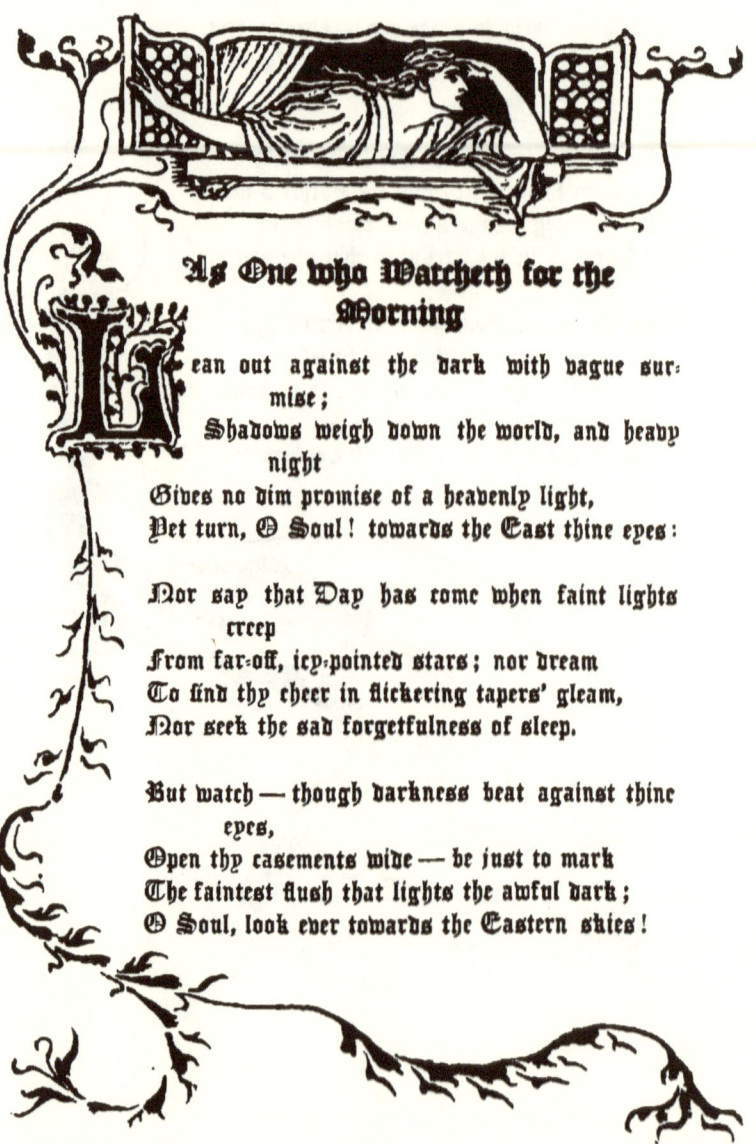

As One who Watcheth for the Morning

Lean out against the dark with vague sur‑
  mise;
  Shadows weigh down the world, and heavy
    night
Gives no dim promise of a heavenly light,
Yet turn, O Soul! towards the East thine eyes:

Nor say that Day has come when faint lights
    creep
From far‑off, icy‑pointed stars; nor dream
To find thy cheer in flickering tapers' gleam,
Nor seek the sad forgetfulness of sleep.

But watch — though darkness beat against thine
    eyes,
Open thy casements wide — be just to mark
The faintest flush that lights the awful dark;
O Soul, look ever towards the Eastern skies!

When Love and Sorrow Meet

Dim in the distance, and scarce recog-
        nized
    By frighted Love's upraised, appealing
        eyes,
Veiled by gray tears, with bended head and
    dumb,
Down through the narrowing weeks does Sor-
    row come, —
Coming too surely, with unfaltering feet
To that appointed day they two shall meet.

In vain, in vain, poor Love, for thee to stay
The hurrying days that push thee on thy way;
In vain for thee to leave thine onward track,
Or thy weak hands to beat strong Sorrow back;
In vain to cry, "Oh, check thine awful pace;"
Still on she comes with veiled and hidden face:

But listen, Love, although she leads white
        Death —
(Oh, listen, Love, and check that sobbing
    breath!)
Beneath her veil of closely falling tears,
Is not the face thy aching heart most fears —

It is not bitter, Love, with frozen pain;
It is not cruel, though thou plead in vain!

On that black day when thou and she shalt
meet,
Her dreaded voice will whisper, clear and sweet,
"Dear Love, though thou must henceforth walk
with me,
My hand shall make all small griefs naught to
thee;
On my true heart with calmness thou shalt bear
All that Life brings to thee of daily care;

"But oh, sweet Love! grant me this gift of
grace —
Push back, dear Love, the veil that hides my
face,
And thou shalt read within my tender eyes
Promise of peace, that now thy fear denies:
Thy Treasure, Love, thy life's sweet joy divine,
Is now, henceforward, to be truly thine.

"Never so truly thine, O Love, before —
Thine, only thine, and thine forevermore!
Death guards thy Treasure till that sure, sweet
day,
To which I 'll lead thee, all the weary way,
When thou shalt enter, too, enduring Rest,
And both be cradled on Death's gentle breast!"

On a Child's Grave
in the Dorchester
Burping-Ground

A hundred years of light and shade,
  And changing hopes and fears,
Have drifted since this grave was made,
  And seen through mists of tears;

So small a grave, and dim with moss,
  And sunk in waving grass,
But mother's heart that's sore with loss,
  Would note it, should she pass.

A hundred years ago he died,
  His very name is not—
The sorrow's buried, tears are dried,
  His life and death's forgot.

Can Love her sacred grief forget?
  Must Love and Grief thus die?
Nay, changed to joy the sharp regret,
  And Love is Life, on high!
Oh worthier Grief that grief should die
  In endless Life and Joy, on high!

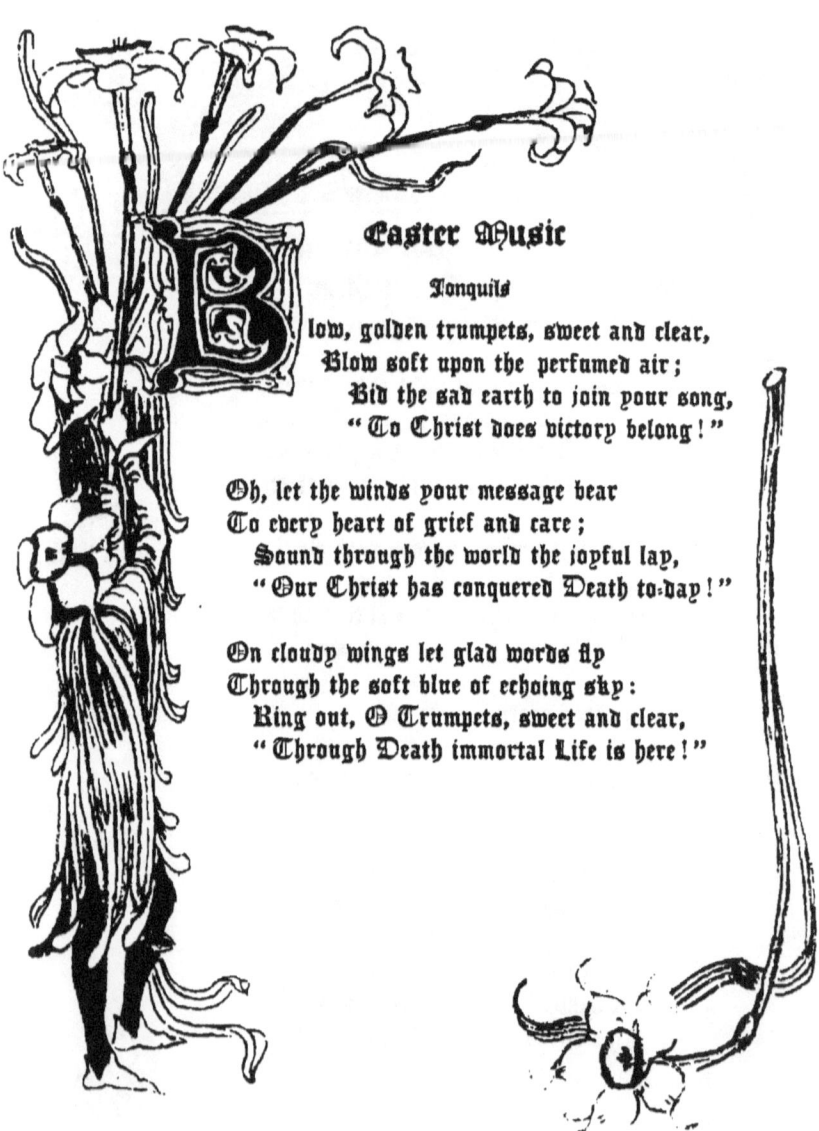

Easter Music

Jonquils

Blow, golden trumpets, sweet and clear,
Blow soft upon the perfumed air;
   Bid the sad earth to join your song,
   "To Christ does victory belong!"

Oh, let the winds your message bear
To every heart of grief and care;
   Sound through the world the joyful lay,
   "Our Christ has conquered Death to-day!"

On cloudy wings let glad words fly
Through the soft blue of echoing sky:
   Ring out, O Trumpets, sweet and clear,
   "Through Death immortal Life is here!"

To the Child of the Sistine Madonna

Through all the mists of years,
　One smiling baby face
Forever young appears,
　Aglow with childish grace!

O questioning sweet eyes,
　O head all golden brown,
Above thee softly lies
　The shadow of a crown.

91

The Message of the Lilies

O quickening life of Easter day,
   O burst of snowy bloom :
"The Lord has risen," Lilies say,
   In gush of sweet perfume !

"Oh, lift your heads and face the sky,
   Oh, watch the brightening dawn ;
For Light, and Life, and Hope are nigh,
   And Death's dark night has gone !

"Up ! up ! to the soft shining blue,
   The freshening wind and sun ;
All Nature thrills, all life is new,
   Christ's victory is won ! "

"Rise, Lord, within our hearts," we cry,
   Through strange, bright mists of tears ;
"Oh, show us 'neath this Easter sky
   Love's own immortal years ! "

Hymn

O patient Christ! when long ago
　　O'er old Judea's rugged hills
Thy willing feet went to and fro,
　　To find and comfort human ills —
Did once thy tender, earnest eyes
Look down the solemn centuries,
And see the smallness of our lives?

Souls struggling for the victory,
　　And martyrs, finding death was gain,
Souls turning from the Truth and Thee,
　　And falling deep in sin and pain —
　　Great heights and depths were surely
　　　　seen,
　　But oh! the dreary waste between —
　　Small lives, not base perhaps, but mean:

Their selfish efforts for the right,
　　Or cowardice that keeps from sin —
Content to only see the height
　　That nobler souls will toil to win!
　　Oh, shame, to think thine eyes should see
　　The souls contented just to be —
　　The lives too small to take in Thee.

Lord, let this thought awake our shame,
  That blessed shame that stings to life,
Rouse us to live for thy dear name,
  Arm us with courage for the strife.
    O Christ! be patient with us still;
    Dear Christ! remember Calvary's hill —
    Our little lives with purpose fill!

To E W W

here is a voice that answers in the
   soul
 When music speaks unto the outer
   ear;
The half of us that longs to be the whole,
The Infinite in mercy drawing near;

Strange gladness that is yet a subtile pain
Holds down the senses, checks the hurried
   breath;
Thought swoons; the human struggles to attain
That harmony of silence we call death!

Verges for Children

The Bird and the Butterfly

For Carrie

hrough the sunny summer sky,
Came a sailing Butterfly:

Wings that seemed with jewels set.
Gleams of rose and violet;

Bars of black in velvet fold
Bright with glints of dusky gold;

Dancing through the sweet sunshine,
Glad with clover's ruddy wine!

Stopping just to gayly sip
The wild pansy's purple lip;

Or to softly swing and rest
On an apple-blossom's breast;

Or to steal the fluffy gold
That the buttercups do hold,

Or to watch the blossoming grass
Ripple, when the light winds pass!

But, still sailing on and on,
Till she finds the sunshine gone;

Frightened then by fading light,
And the softly gathering Night,

She would chase the flying Day,
So she stops to ask the way —

Lights upon a swinging nest,
"Right or left? which way is West?"

And a young Bird answers low —
"On — towards the sunset's glow!

"But just say, before you fly,
Is it beautiful — the sky?

"Shall I see it, do you know?
Tell me that, before you go!"

So, ere her bright wings she spread,
This is what she softly said:

"Yes, oh yes! on some glad dawn,
When Night's stars are dimmed and gone,

" Look straight up into the sky,
Fearless spread your wings — then, Fly ! "

So she fluttered from the nest,
Seeking still the yellow West !

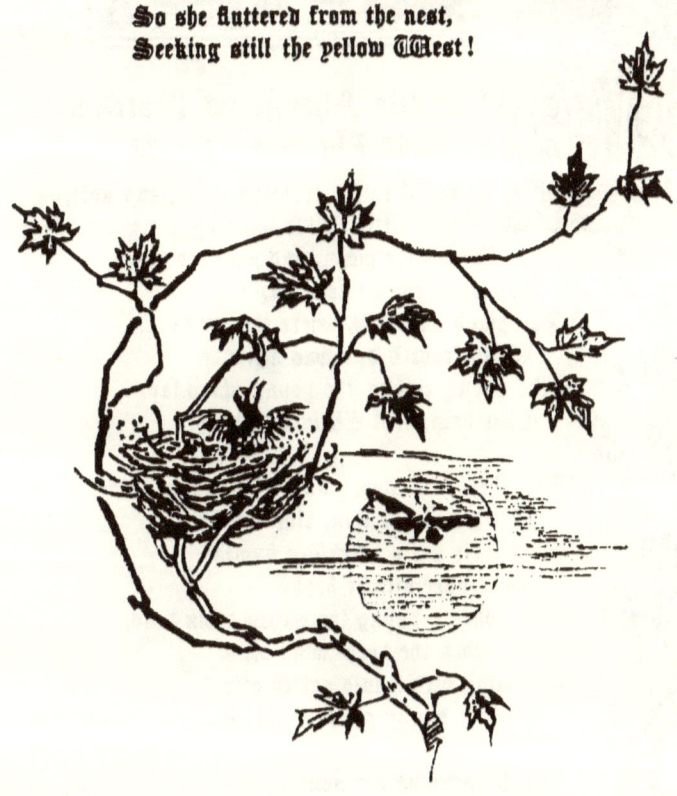

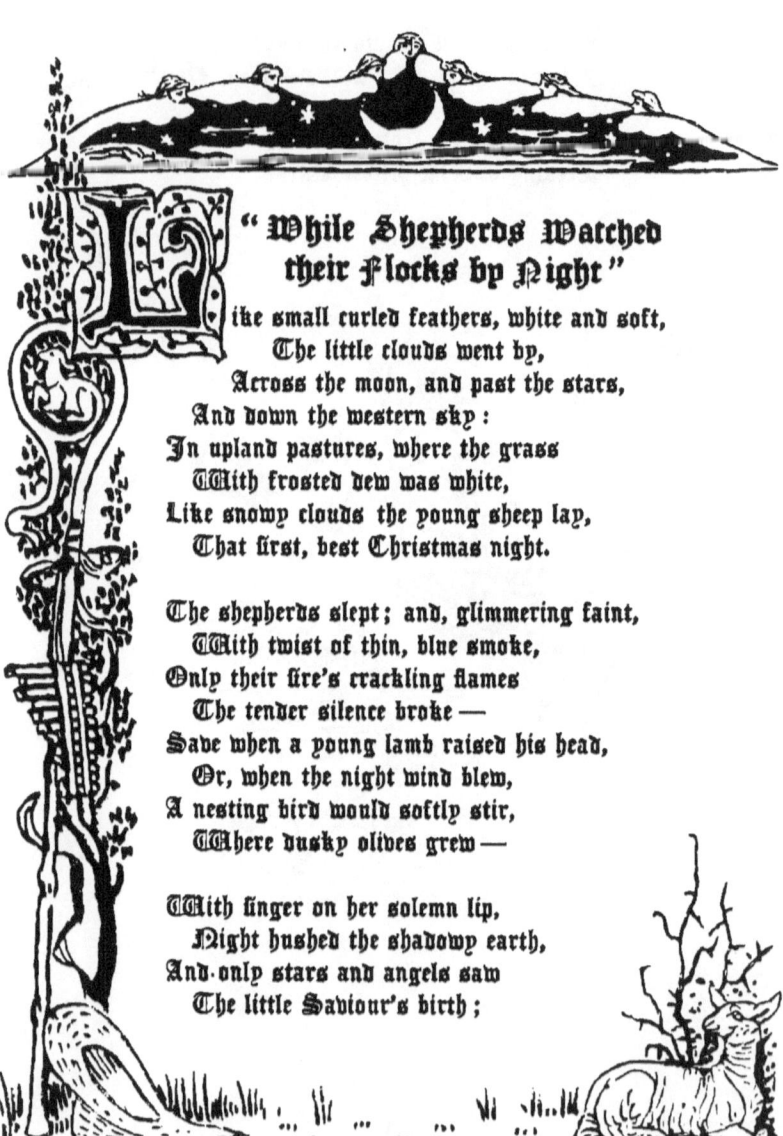

"While Shepherds Watched their Flocks by Night"

Like small curled feathers, white and soft,
　　The little clouds went by,
　　Across the moon, and past the stars,
And down the western sky:
In upland pastures, where the grass
　　With frosted dew was white,
Like snowy clouds the young sheep lay,
　　That first, best Christmas night.

The shepherds slept; and, glimmering faint,
　　With twist of thin, blue smoke,
Only their fire's crackling flames
　　The tender silence broke —
Save when a young lamb raised his head,
　　Or, when the night wind blew,
A nesting bird would softly stir,
　　Where dusky olives grew —

With finger on her solemn lip,
　　Night hushed the shadowy earth,
And only stars and angels saw
　　The little Saviour's birth;

Then came such flash of silver light
    Across the bending skies,
The wondering shepherds woke, and hid
    Their frightened, dazzled eyes!

And all their gentle sleepy flock
    Looked up, then slept again,
Nor knew the light that dimmed the stars
    Brought endless Peace to men —
Nor even heard the gracious words
    That down the ages ring —
" The Christ is born! the Lord has come,
    Good=will on earth to bring! "

Then o'er the moonlit, misty fields,
    Dumb with the world's great joy,
The shepherds sought the white=walled town,
    Where lay the baby boy —
And oh, the gladness of the world,
    The glory of the skies,
Because the longed=for Christ looked up
    In Mary's happy eyes!

Bossy and the Daisy

Right up into Bossy's eyes,
    Looked the Daisy, boldly,
But, alas! to his surprise,
    Bossy ate him, coldly.

Listen! Daisies in the fields,
    Hide away from Bossy!
Daisies make the milk she yields,
    And her coat grow glossy.

So, each day, she tries to find
    Daisies nodding sweetly,
And although it's most unkind,
    Bites their heads off, neatly!

The Dance of the Fairies

IN my garden, in the midnight,
In the misty shining moonlight,
    Stand the lilies, swaying, bending,
Half afraid that they are lending,
By their sweet looks and sedate,
Countenance to hours so late.
    (Yet they give a sidelong glance,
At the Fairies' airy dance!)

        O'er the grass,
        Hand in hand,
        Kiss and pass,
        Fairy Band—

        Round about
        With the breeze,
        In and out
        'Neath the trees!

        Flow'r bells ring,
        With soft chime,
        Fairies sing,
        Keeping time—

On they go,
   Stepping soft,
Laughing low,
   Kissing oft.

Steps so light
   Scarcely make
Dew-drops bright
   Gleam and shake!

Yet my stately lilies wear
Such a disapproving air,
   Looking down with sweet heads bent
   On the Fairy Parliament,
Trusting their white dignity
Flippant Fays may chance to see.
   (Yet I think, from their shy glance,
   They would like to join the dance!)

The Fairies' Shopping

Where do you think the Fairies go
  To buy their blankets ere the snow?

When Autumn comes, with frosty days,
The sorry shivering little Fays

Begin to think it's time to creep
Down to their caves for Winter sleep.

But first they come from far and near
To buy, where shops are not too dear,

(The wind and frost bring prices down,
So Fall's their time to come to town!)

Where on the hill-side rough and steep
Browse all day long the cows and sheep,

The mullein's yellow candles burn
Over the heads of dry sweet fern:

All summer long the mullein weaves
His soft and thick and woolly leaves,

Warmer blankets were never seen
Than these broad leaves of fuzzy green —

(The cost of each is but a shekel
Made from the gold of honeysuckle!)

To buy their sheets and fine white lace
(With which to trim a pillow-case),

They only have to go next door,
Where stands a sleek brown spider's store,

And there they find the misty threads
Ready to cut into sheets and spreads;

Then for a pillow, pluck with care
Some soft-winged seeds as light as air;

Just what they want the thistle brings,
But thistles are such surly things —

And so, though it is somewhat high,
The clematis the Fairies buy.

The only bedsteads that they need
Are silky pods of ripe milk-weed,

With hangings of the dearest things —
Autumn leaves, or butterflies' wings!

And dandelions' fuzzy heads
They use to stuff their feather beds;

And yellow snapdragons supply
The nightcaps that the Fairies buy,

To which some blades of grass they pin,
And tie them 'neath each little chin.

Then, shopping done, the Fairies cry,
"Our Summer's gone! oh sweet, good-bye!"

And sadly to their caves they go,
To hide away from Winter's snow —

And then, though winds and storms may beat,
The Fairies' sleep is warm and sweet!

The Buttercup

O

h bravely she holds up,
    To catch the sun and dew,
    And sometimes raindrops, too,
Her tiny golden cup.

She needs the clouds and rain,
    To make her brightest flowers,
    For her life, just as ours,
Can grow because of pain!

110

Night

The tender Night, in sable dress,
Leans o'er the earth, intent to bless;

Like a round ball of misty light
Her lantern moon glows soft and bright;

The yellow stars that wink and pawn
Are her small candles till the dawn:

Thus lighted, round the world she goes,
To heal with sleep its sharpest woes!

The tears Day brought, Night gently dries,
With her soft touch on weary eyes —

In mists of dreams each tired brain
Forgets its trouble or its pain —

To Age she brings back youth and joy,
The gray-haired man becomes a boy!

Fair visions of the Youth she shows
Of all the Future may disclose:

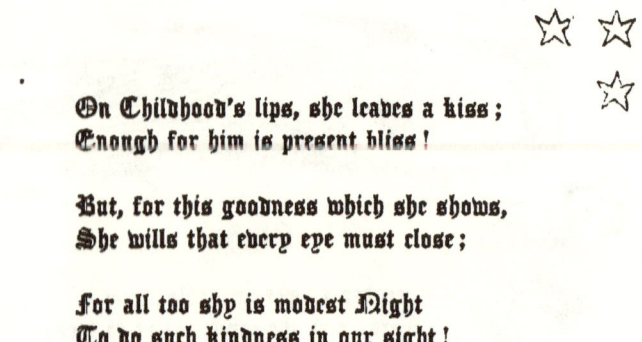

On Childhood's lips, she leaves a kiss;
Enough for him is present bliss!

But, for this goodness which she shows,
She wills that every eye must close;

For all too shy is modest Night
To do such kindness in our sight!

Polly

The tufted grass is bright with dew
  That damps her gown and wets her
    shoe,
    As through it Polly gayly trips
  With ruddy cheeks and smiling lips!
By Love and Duty both she's led
When hast'ning to the milking-shed—
  The patient cows with gentle eyes
  Will show no grave or stern surprise,
If, ere her work she does begin
Her sweetheart Jem a kiss shall win!

The Waits

AT the break of Christmas Day,
    Through the frosty starlight ringing,
Faint and sweet and far away,
Comes the sound of children, singing,
    Chanting, singing,
        "Cease to mourn,
        For Christ is born,
    Peace and joy to all men bringing!"

Careless that the chill winds blow,
    Growing stronger, sweeter, clearer,
Noiseless footfalls in the snow
    Bring the happy voices nearer;
        Hear them singing,
        "Winter's drear,
        But Christ is here,
    Mirth and gladness with Him bringing!"

"Merry Christmas!" hear them say,
    As the East is growing lighter;
"May the joy of Christmas Day
    Make your whole year gladder, brighter!"
        Join their singing,
        "To each home
        Our Christ has come,
    All Love's treasures with Him bringing!"

114